Isabelle Harper

MY CATS
NICK & NORA

Illustrated by Barry Moser

THE BLUE SKY PRESS

An Imprint of Scholastic Inc. • New York

THE BLUE SKY PRESS

For information regarding permission, please write to:
Permissions Department,
The Blue Sky Press, an imprint of Scholastic Inc.,
555 Broadway, New York, NY 10012

The Blue Sky Press is a trademark of Scholastic Inc.

Izzy, Emmie, and Barry wish to thank Friskies Pet Care, a division
of Nestlé/Carnation Food Company, as well as MILK-BONE, a division
of Nabisco, Inc., for permission to use their pet food in this book.
Friskies is a registered trademark of Nestlé Inc.
MILK-BONE® is a registered trademark of Nabisco, Inc.

Library of Congress Cataloging-in-Publication Data
Harper, Isabelle.
My cats Nick and Nora / Isabelle Harper & Barry Moser.
p.   cm.
Summary: Two young girls spend a day with two spirited cats.
ISBN 0-590-47620-3
[1. Cats — Fiction.] I. Moser, Barry, ill. II. Title.
PZ7.H23133Mw   1995   [E] — dc20   94-31981   CIP   AC

12 11 10 9 8 7 6 5 4 3 2 1   5 6 7 8 9/9 0/0

Printed in Singapore

First printing, September 1995

The illustrations in this book were executed with watercolor on paper
handmade by Simon Green at the Barcham Green Mills in Maidstone,
Kent, Great Britain, especially for the Royal Watercolor Society.
Production supervision by Angela Biola
Art direction by Kathleen Westray
Designed by Barry Moser

For Sam, Mehitabel, Rufus, Tweed, Big Momma, Smokey, Calhoun, Jenny-Any-Dots,
Minnie-One-Dot, Curtis, Dusty & Toasty, Yard Boss, and
all the other wonderful cats who have graced our lives

EVERY SUNDAY when my cousin Emmie comes over
to my house, the first thing we do is go find Nick and Nora.

It isn't always easy.

They have lots of places to hide.

But no matter where they hide,
we always find them.

We give them their lessons . . .

. . . and because today is their birthday,
we make them look especially nice.

We invite all their friends . . .

. . . and have a birthday party.

After the party, we take Nick and Nora for a walk.

Our neighbor Fluffy sees us.

He wasn't invited to the party because he's not nice.

He likes to fight.

And sometimes Nick and Nora are not nice,
either, no matter how pretty they look.

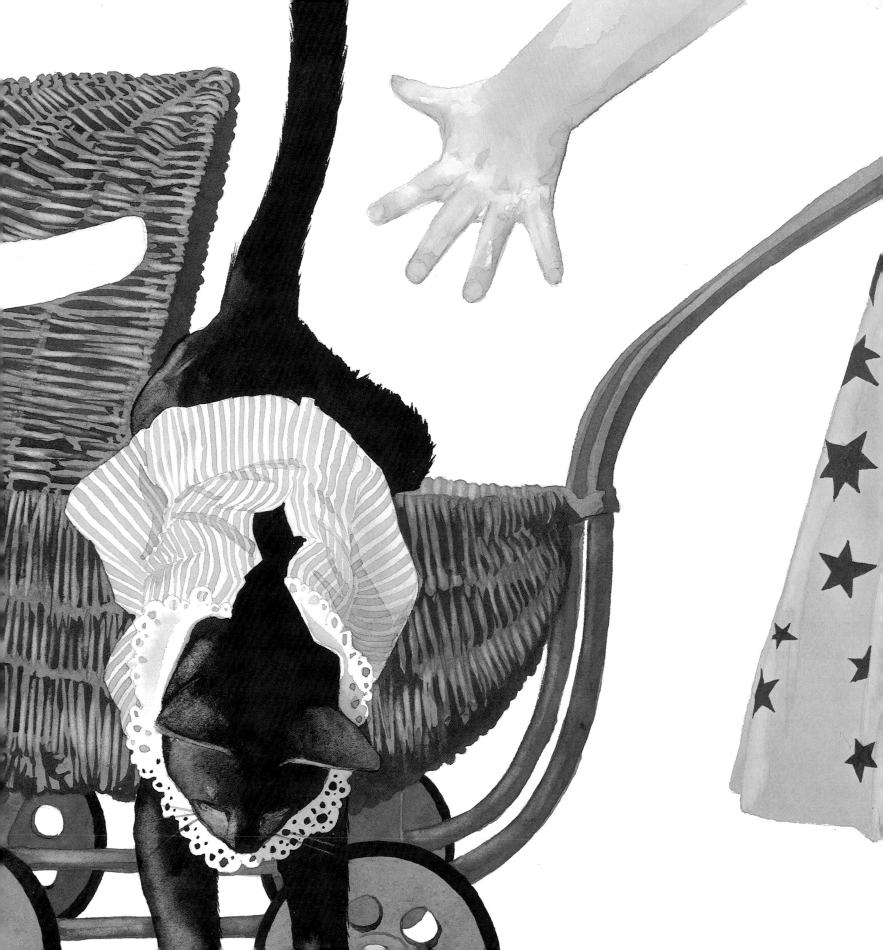

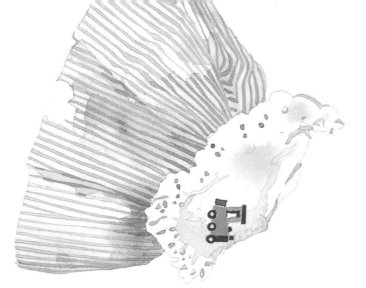

This isn't the first time Fluffy has ruined our Sunday afternoon walk.

Emmie and I go back to my house.
We don't see Nick or Nora anywhere.

But we're not worried. We know exactly
what will bring them home.

And when Nick and Nora do come back, we can see they are tired and ready for their nap.

And so are we.